Ant and Grasshopper

Ant and Grasshopper

written by
Luli Gray

illustrated by
Giuliano Ferri

MARGARET K. MCELDERRY BOOKS • New York London Toronto Sydney

MARGARET K. McELDERRY BOOKS
An imprint of Simon & Schuster Children's Publishing Division
1230 Avenue of the Americas, New York, New York 10020
Text copyright © 2011 by Luli Gray
Illustrations copyright © 2011 by Giuliano Ferri
All rights reserved, including the right of reproduction in whole or in part in any form.
MARGARET K. McELDERRY BOOKS is a trademark of Simon & Schuster, Inc.
For information about special discounts for bulk purchases, please contact Simon &
Schuster Special Sales at 1-866-506-1949 or business@simonandschuster.com.
The Simon & Schuster Speakers Bureau can bring authors to your live event. For more
information or to book an event, contact the Simon & Schuster Speakers Bureau
at 1-866-248-3049 or visit our website at www.simonspeakers.com.
Book design by Lauren Rille
The text for this book is set in Celestia Antiqua.
The illustrations for this book are rendered in watercolor and colored pencil on Arches
watercolor paper.
Manufactured in China
1210 SCP
10 9 8 7 6 5 4 3 2 1
Cataloging-in-Publication Data is available from the Library of Congress.
ISBN 978-1-4169-5140-7 (hardcover)

FIRST
EDITION

In loving memory of my accountant and friend, Jack Gottlieb, and to Bonnie Layman, who would never leave a hungry hoppergrass out in the cold.—L. G.

To my little Miriam,
with hopes that she will always have her desire to sing.—G. F.

A nt was rich. His house was very grand, with many rooms, and the storeroom was his favorite. All through the spring and summer he worked hard gathering things to eat for the winter, and every afternoon he went to the storeroom to count them.

By June he had 947 beans, 28 raisins, and a fine smelly wedge of yellow cheese.

"Nine hundred forty-five," he counted. "Nine hundred forty-six, nine hundred forty-seven."

Then he took exactly three bites of cheese.

"Dee-lishus!" he said,
and began to count his raisins.

One day as he sat counting, he heard a noise.
"Shhh!" he said. "I'm counting!"
The noise went on and on. Ant opened the door, and there on his lawn stood a grasshopper, playing a fiddle.

"Well, I never!" said Ant.

"Well, I always," said Grasshopper.

"It's June, Ant! The sun is warm; the sky is blue. Come out and dance—I'll play for you!"

"Humph!" said Ant. "You should be storing up food for the winter, not fiddling around, wasting time."

All summer long Ant worked hard. Every afternoon he counted his beans, and his raisins, and his cheese. And all summer long he heard Grasshopper playing his fiddle and singing.

October came, with bright leaves tumbling on a breeze that carried a promise of winter. Ant sat fidgeting at his desk, trying to add up his accounts. But his pen kept making swans out of the twos and fat snowmen out of the eights, and the numbers hopped around in his head, refusing to settle down.

"Come ye thankful creatures, come, sing a song of harvest home. All is safely gathered in, ere the winter storms begin," sang Grasshopper, peeking in the window.

"Oh, hush!"

said Ant, yanking down the shade.

October came, with bright leaves tumbling on a breeze that carried a promise of winter. Ant sat fidgeting at his desk, trying to add up his accounts. But his pen kept making swans out of the twos and fat snowmen out of the eights, and the numbers hopped around in his head, refusing to settle down.

"Come ye thankful creatures, come, sing a song of harvest home. All is safely gathered in, ere the winter storms begin," sang Grasshopper, peeking in the window.

"Oh, hush!"

said Ant, yanking down the shade.

September came. It was harvest time, and Ant added to his rich store. He had 604 kernels of corn, 72 peanuts, and a piece of ham bigger than he was.

"Dee-lishus and noo-trishus!" he said.

Sometimes the music got into Ant's head
and made him lose count.
"Twenty-four, no, twenty-six—oh,
**drat
that
hoppergrass!"**

"Six hundred four kernels of corn, gathered on a summer
morn. No! No! No! Seven ounces of ham, yes ma'am . . .
Oh, for heaven's sake, what is wrong with me?"
He heard a tap-tap-tapping and flung open the door.

"Oh, Ant, let me in, there's a good fellow.
It's getting cold and I'm sooo hungry!"

"Ha!" said Ant. "I knew it was you, with your fiddle-dee-doo! I warned you. You danced and sang all summer, while respectable folk worked hard for a living, and it serves you right. Good night!" And he slammed the door and went back to counting.

November blew in, cold and blustery. "**Wooooo!**" cried the wind, rattling the windows while Ant paced back and forth. "I'm sure I don't know what's gotten into me," he muttered. He sat down by the fire, watching the flames dance up the chimney.

"I wonder . . . ," said Ant. "I wish . . ."
The clock struck ten:

bong,
bong,
bong,
bong,
bong,
bong,
bong,
bong,
bong,
bong.

Ant went to bed.

But fragments of rhyme and wisps of music jangled about in his head, and he thrashed and kicked till the bedclothes were all a-tangle. When at last he fell asleep, he dreamed he stood on a stage before a great crowd that shouted,

"Play!
Dance!
Sing!"

And he couldn't play a note or dance a dance. He opened his mouth to sing, but there wasn't one song in him, no song at all.

"I can't! I'm an ant!"

"Boo!" roared the crowd.

"Boo!"

The cold, hateful booing blew Ant right out of bed with a bump, and he woke up. The night had grown quiet. *Too quiet*, thought Ant. He ran to the door, and there on the step lay Grasshopper, barely visible under a thick layer of snow.

"Grasshopper, is that you?" said Ant. "What are you doing? Get up! Go home!"

"D-D-D-Don't h-h-have a h-h-home," said Grasshopper, his teeth chattering.

"No home!" exclaimed Ant. "I never heard of such a thing!" After a moment, Ant dragged Grasshopper into the house, where he laid him by the fire in the second best peanut shell.

"C-C-C-Cold!" Grasshopper said, shivering.

"Oh, yes indeed, poor fellow, have some hot cider," said Ant.

But Grasshopper was shivering too hard to swallow.

"Here," said Ant. "Here are five dee-lishus beans and three bites of noo-trishus cheese and two-more-lishus raisins."

But Grasshopper was shivering too hard to eat.

Ant tucked a dandelion-down quilt around Grasshopper.
"I didn't know," Ant said. "I had no idea. I didn't mean . . ."

Grasshopper's eyes opened and he looked up at Ant.
"Hallo, Ant," he said. "Ahhhhh-choo!"

"Bless you!" said Ant, wiping the sneeze off his face.
"Bless you," said Grasshopper. "Did I hear you mention
beans and raisins?"

All through the winter, Grasshopper stayed with Ant, playing and singing every evening when Ant was done counting. One evening, as the old year drew to a close, the two friends sat by the fire.

"One thousand, one hundred, and forty-two," said Ant, closing the account book with a sigh. "Sometimes," he said, "sometimes I wish I could sing. Just a bit, you know."

"Sing?" said Grasshopper. "Anyone can sing. But working hard and counting are splendid things! Why, you saved my life with your eleventy jillion beans, raisins, and corn!"

"One thousand, one hundred, and forty-two, actually," said Ant. "Including peanuts. But anyone can count."

"Not me," said Grasshopper. He played a chord on his fiddle. "Do you know 'Here We Come a Waffle-ing'?" He sang it three times through, and then, rather shyly and (to tell the truth) quite off-key, Ant joined in.

Here we come a waffle-ing

With syrup and with jam,

Here we come to dance a jig,

And eat a lot of ham.

Pizza joy come to you,

Made of pickles, mice, and glue,

And we wish you and squish you a happy New Year,

And we wish you a happy New Year!

"I wish I could sing like you," said Ant.

"I love the way you sing!" said Grasshopper.

"I wish I could *count*!"

"Oh, Grasshopper," said Ant.

"Everybody counts."